GOD CHANGES US
A 5-week Bible Study

Cherri S. Wheeler

TABLE OF CONTETNS

FOREWORD

Do you ever feel that your mistakes limit what you can do for the kingdom of God? Are you struggling with feeling unworthy of God's forgiveness?

Do you feel stuck?

In a world where our mistakes often feel final, this Bible study on transformation offers a timely and hope-filled perspective on God's incredible ability to redeem every misstep. Through engaging lessons and thoughtful reflection, readers are guided to see how the broken pieces of our lives are never wasted in God's hands—they are recycled and repurposed for His kingdom purposes.

This study beautifully illustrates that our failures can become the foundation for new strengths, and our regrets can be transformed into testimonies of grace. With biblical wisdom and practical applications, it reminds us that no journey is too messy for God's restoration. Whether you're seeking personal renewal or longing to encourage others, this resource will inspire you to trust God's transforming power and embrace the repurposed attributes he is cultivating in your life.

I wholeheartedly recommend this Bible study to anyone who desires to experience true spiritual transformation and discover the purpose that comes from allowing God to turn every misstep into a stepping stone for His glory. You, too, can get unstuck.

Rev. Betsy Haas

Ordained United Methodist minister

Author of *Mourning Break, ADVENTuring to the Manger, Psalms by the Sea,* and *ReLENTless Devotion*

ABOUT THE AUTHOR

Cherri S. Wheeler is a retired United States Air Force Chaplain who served her country for over 31 years. After retirement, she continues in ministry, serving several local agencies as a volunteer chaplain. She provides pulpit supply for churches across North Carolina. She serves as the State Team Leader in Logistics for North Carolina Baptist on Mission, Disaster Response. She has served as an Adjunct Instructor at Denver Seminary, teaching Doctoral Students in the Leadership Track and was First Reader for two doctoral students.

Her education includes a Bachelor of Science degree in Education from Southeastern Oklahoma State University, 1982; a Master of Divinity from Southwestern Baptist Theological Seminary, 1985; and a Doctor of Ministry from Denver Seminary, 2006.

Since their retirement from the military in 2015, Cherri and her husband, Wade, have lived in Southern Shores, NC. They enjoy golfing and you will find them on the course on any given day when not responding to natural disasters around the state and nation.

ACKNOWLEDGEMENTS

This Bible study would not be possible without my "village" of supporters. First, I want to thank God who inspired this study and wouldn't let me ignore his calling to write it. (God knows how much I really did not want to do this.) Second, my husband, Wade, who for over 39 years has been my biggest supporter. He has supported all my crazy callings because he knew they came after much prayer.

I am thankful to Marilyn Penland for her faithful leadership of hundreds of women's Bible studies and prayer groups through the years. She and her ladies were my first beta test of the materials. They found a couple of my mistakes and suggested the glossary of terms and biographical sketches of the four case studies. My second beta test was a smaller number of Christian women I have met through my husband's class reunions, whom I respect. Patricia Gillette and Theresa Wilson provided even deeper insights into how the study had challenged and strengthened them in their own faith journey. They also offered incredible insight into some of my examples and questions. Finally, I was so encouraged by Rev Betsy Haas, a published Christian writer, who showed enthusiasm toward my Bible study and insights into the publishing world were most appreciated. Her encouragement reignited my desire to see this through publishing.

To Yvonne Sternberg, my grammarian expert. From the first draft to the published piece, her advice, counsel, and red pen were always helpful, though sometimes painful. Her love for English and correct writing styles shone as she has helped me stay laser focused.

Those mentioned above gave wise counsel and noted needed corrections. If there are mistakes, they are mine and mine alone.

Thank you all for helping make this work a reality.

INTRODUCTION

The idea for this study came during Advent of 2023. Recovering from back surgery, a Care Team member from my church brought me the devotional by Sarah Young, entitled, Jesus Listens for Advent & Christmas – Prayers for the Season. A line from the book resonated deeply with me, a line from her prayer, "You have shown me that even my mistakes and sins can be recycled into something good—through your transformational grace."[1] I had never thought of God's love and grace in those terms. It turned on end my understanding of Paul's declaration, "And we know that in all things God works for the good of those who love him, who are called according to his purpose" (Romans 8:28).[2] My belief, for as long as I can remember, had God blotting out my mistakes and sins, as in "as far as the east is from the west, so far has he removed our transgressions from us" (Psalm 103:12). Yet, this nuance of recycling my transgressions into something new, different, and usable began to set me free. For whatever reason, I believed that my mistakes limited what I could do for the kingdom of God. I believed I had short-circuited God's plan for my life, and I was providing only an "honorable mention" effort to the work of the kingdom. That which I saw as a limitation to my effectiveness, God is now showing me he is ever transforming me for the work he has for me.

In the pages that follow, my prayer for you is that you will find God's transformational love and grace liberating and freeing. Too often we are convinced in our own minds that we are not worthy of forgiveness for the mistakes we make. We have been convinced by friends, family, and society that we have to get cleaned up and straightened up before we can come before God or be used by him. The church itself has done little to dispel this fallacy. Those of us in the church have amnesia to our own brokenness and failures and have become haughty toward those who enter our buildings looking different, smelling different, and acting different; those who "don't measure up" to our standards.

This study is for both those who are in the church and those who are not, those who are Christians and those who are seekers. Some of the information will be familiar; some will challenge preconceived ideas and long-held beliefs. I pray you will enter this study, seeking change, real change – transformational change. I pray you will allow God to enter in with you through this journey, and you will be transparent with God and with yourself. I pray you will welcome God's transformational love to redeem, restore, repurpose, and recycle your life.

Best Regards,
Cherri Wheeler

---

[1] Young, Sarah. Jesus Listens for Advent & Christmas Prayers for the Season, Thomas Nelson, 2023, pg. 54.
[2] Unless otherwise noted, Scripture quotations taken from the Holy Bible, New International Version, NIV.

GLOSSARY OF TERMS

Definitions of concepts and terminology used in this study.

1. **Epistle:** A term denoting letters written to individuals or churches in the New Testament. There are 21 Epistles in the New Testament (Romans – Jude). Paul the Apostle wrote most of the letters.

2. **Gospel:** At its basic definition means good news. Biblically, the gospel is used to share the news of salvation in and through Jesus Christ as foretold in the Prophetic writings.

3. **Gospels:** When referring to the first four books of the New Testament, they refer to the work of God through his son Jesus, the Christ. Some have described the Gospels as biographies, which is not fully correct. Though there is some biographical material about Jesus' birth and early childhood, the rest of the material relates only to the three years of Jesus' earthly ministry.

4. **Levite:** A descendant of Levi, one of the 12 sons of Jacob, who made up the tribes of Israel. The Levites were set apart by God to be the priests of the people of Israel. Levites were charged with offering sacrifices, leading the people in worship and confession. Only the Levites who were direct descendants of Aaron were allowed in the most sacred portion of the Temple; all other Levites were assigned to assist in the running of the Temple. Levites were not assigned an inheritance of land; rather, they were given cities within the other tribal areas in which they ministered to the people.

5. **Pharisees:** Understood as "separated ones." It is a term that describes both a religious and a political party during Jesus' time in ministry. Pharisees believed Jews should strictly adhere to the laws of God. Pharisees believed that since many Jews and all Gentiles did not keep a strict adherence to the law, Pharisees limited their exposure to such people and considered them as sinners. They believed in the resurrection of the dead. In Jesus' day, the Pharisees seemed to be held in good esteem by most Jews. They also believed firmly in the importance of tradition, holding it as equal to the law. Pharisees were also called scribes.

6. **Redemption:** In the New Testament, redemption is what God does through his son, Jesus. Redemption refers to the payment made on our behalf for our sins. The cost of sin is the separation (eternally) from God. The only way to be redeemed from our sins was for a perfect sacrifice to be offered in our place. God provided that redeemer in Jesus, who was without sin. Jesus paid a debt he did not owe for those who had a debt they could not pay.

7. **Reuel (friend of God):** In Exodus 2 was a priest in Midian. Moses after fleeing Egypt finds himself in Midian where he intervenes on behalf of Reuel's seven daughters who were trying to water their flocks.

The daughters returned home earlier than usual. Reuel asks his daughters why they were home early. They explained that an Egyptian had watered their flocks. Reuel sends them back to invite the man to dinner. Later in Exodus 3, it says this man, now referred to as Jethro, was Moses' father-in-law who had given Zipporah to Moses as his wife. She gave birth to two sons.

8. **Sadducees:** Were Jews often from the aristocracy in Jesus' time. They were wealthy, landowners, and often merchants. Those of the Sadducees adamantly opposed Jesus' ministry and did not believe in a resurrection of the dead. Sadducees rejected both oral and written tradition that dominated the Pharisaical sect, believing that the Law of Moses was the only binding law.

9. **Salvation:** Used in the Old Testament means deliverance from danger or trouble. In the New Testament, salvation refers to deliverance from eternal damnation through the birth, life, death, and resurrection of Jesus, God's only Son. To receive salvation one must believe what the Bible teaches about Jesus, repent of one's sins, and follow in faith God's precepts.

10. **Sanhedrin:** The ruling body and court of justice among the Jews during Jesus' ministry. The Sanhedrin was headed by the high priest of Israel. It was also known as the council or the assembly (depending on the translation of the Bible one uses). The Sanhedrin had limited authority over religious, civil, and criminal matters based on the ruling foreign nation that dominated the region. During Jesus's ministry, the foreign nation in control was the Roman government. The Sanhedrin was made up of the chief priest, elders, and scribes. The Sanhedrin had 71 members.

BIOGRAPHIES OF BIBLICAL EXAMPLES

1.   **King Saul (1 Samuel 8–31 and 2 Samuel 1).** Saul is the first king of the Israelites. A king was demanded by the people due to the corruption of Samuel's two sons whom he appointed as judges. Samuel was the chief priest at the time. Samuel's sons, Joel and Abijah, took bribes and perverted justice (1 Samuel 8:3, NASB). God warned the people through Samuel about the problems with having a human king versus God ruling over them, yet the people still demanded a king. Saul was from the tribe of Benjamin. He was handsome and stood taller than most men. Samuel anoints Saul as king just as God told him to do. Saul was 40 years old when he began his reign. The people accepted him as their king and saw him as their deliverer from their enemies.

Saul was victorious in battles early in his reign. Saul then decided he would go against the Law of Moses, as spoken by God, taking on the role of priest offering burnt offerings in Samuel's absence. Samuel confronted Saul regarding his foolish behavior. Because of this act of disobedience, Samuel communicates that Saul's reign would not endure. Saul's disobedience continued, prompting God to remove his hand of protection from him hand of protection from him. Eventually, Saul dies on the battlefield, having been mortally wounded by the Philistines. Yet he took his own life rather than be captured and abused by the Philistines.

During Saul's reign, God removes his hand from him and has Samuel anoint David, son of Jesse to be king. There was an extended period when Saul actively pursued David to kill him but never accomplished it due to God's protection of David.

2.   King David (1 Samuel 16–31, 2 Samuel, 1 Kings 1–2, many Psalms). David, the youngest son of Jesse, was from Bethlehem, a descendant of the tribe of Judah. He was a shepherd, a musician, and a songwriter (Psalms). He worked under King Saul as a musician to help soothe Saul after God removed his blessing from him. David was also Saul's armor-bearer. David took on Goliath and won the fight with his slingshot. He and Saul's son, Jonathan, became fast friends, even after Saul tried to kill David on several occasions. Saul's jealousy of David's successes was at issue. (1 Samuel 21:11b, "Saul has slain his thousands, and David his tens of thousands.").

David was a warrior and as he sought God, his success on the battlefield was impressive. However, one spring for reasons unexplained in the scriptures, David did not lead his army into battle. In his restlessness, he went to the rooftop of the palace and saw Bathsheba bathing. That encounter led David into adultery, lies, plots, betrayal and finally, the murder of Uriah, the Hittite; one of David's mighty men. From there, life became much more difficult for him. The baby conceived from his adulterous affair died. Absalom, one of his sons, attempted a coup, which left David's nation and family divided.

As David's life neared its end, there was another attempt to usurp the kingship by Adonijah, David's son, setting himself up as King; however, David did not allow Adonijah's kingship to stand and instead, had Solomon anointed as his successor by Nathan the prophet and Zadok the priest.

David's heart's desire was to build a permanent Temple in Jerusalem for God, but it was not allowed since David had been a warrior and was responsible for the deaths of so many of his enemies. It was Solomon, David's son by Bathsheba, who built the magnificent Temple for God.

3.   Moses (Exodus–Deuteronomy). Moses, the son of Levite parents (the priestly clan), was destined to be used of God from his birth. He was born at a time when the Pharaoh who arose to power realized how large a number the Hebrew people were and did not realize it was Joseph, a son of Jacob, a Hebrew, who had saved Egypt from a seven-year drought. Rather than treat the Hebrews as allies, he feared them and questioned their allegiance. Due to the Pharaoh's fear, he ordered the Hebrews into slavery. He wanted their number reduced but when that didn't happen under the cruel conditions of slavery, he decided to order all male babies killed at birth. Even that aggressive order did not thwart God's plan. When Moses was born, his parents hid him, then put him in a basket and placed him in the Nile River, where Pharaoh's daughter found him. Moses was raised in the Pharaoh's household and received an education and privilege.

At the age of 40, he went out to see what was happening with the Hebrew people. He witnessed a Hebrew slave being abused by an Egyptian. Taking matters into his own hands, he killed the Egyptian, burying him in the desert. The Pharaoh burned with anger over what had happened, which caused Moses to flee to Midian. For another 40 years, he worked alongside Jethro, who became his father-in-law, shepherding sheep and raising a family. It was in the desert setting that Moses encountered God through the burning bush. God called Moses to free the Hebrew people from their bondage and take them back to the promised land in Canaan.

Though Moses did not accept his call willingly, he did approach Pharaoh asking for permission to take the Hebrew people out into the desert to sacrifice to their God. Each request was met with a resounding no. Each no answer was met with plagues that God sent on the Egyptians but not the Hebrews. Finally, the Hebrew people were allowed to cross the Red Sea on dry land. Followed by the Egyptians, who reneged on their permission but were decimated when the sea closed over them.

Moses was given the 10 commandments; he led the people to the promised land. Moses sent spies into the land. Ten of the twelve spies reported that the people were too strong for the Hebrews to defeat. They even incited their tribes to reject going into the land God had promised. The people rejected God's promise to turn the land over to them. Their disobedience caused them to wander in the wilderness for a generation (40 years) until all those who were adults were deceased, not including Joshua and Caleb, who had encouraged the people to enter the promised land.

The 40 years of wandering saw many miracles and lots of grumbling by the people. Even Moses grew weary with all the issues that arose. Unfortunately for Moses, he disobeyed God the second time water was needed. Rather than call out the water from the rock as God had commanded, he hit the rock with his staff as he had been commanded the first time they needed water. Water came, but the consequence for Moses' disobedience was that he would not enter the promised land. However, God did allow him to see it from afar.

4. Saul/Paul (Acts of the Apostles and most of the New Testament Letters). Saul was the Hebrew name given to him since his parents were Hebrew, and he was given the name Paul a Greek name since his parents were also Roman citizens. He was from the city of Tarsus. Saul attended the best Rabbinical schools, studying under the great Rabbis of the day. Saul was from the tribe of Benjamin, he was a Pharisee. Saul was at Stephen's stoning and approved of what took place. Saul began his reign of terror, seizing men and women, who were Christians, from their homes and putting them in prison. Saul went to the high priest seeking letters authorizing him to bring Christians from Damascus to Jerusalem and into prison.

On his way to Damascus, Saul had an encounter with the resurrected Jesus and was blinded, confronted about his persecution of Christ's followers, and is taken to Damascus by his traveling companions. There he is approached by Ananias, a disciple of Christ, who explains Jesus' ministry, death, and resurrection. At that point, Saul repents and prays for forgiveness. Saul regains his sight. He was introduced to the believers in Damascus and he began preaching in the synagogues that Jesus is the Son of God. Saul's new zeal for Christ was met with threats on his life. After several more issues with Jews trying to end Saul's life, he reached out to the non-Jewish communities. Saul went to Jerusalem and was met by the other apostles, who were reluctant to speak with him until Barnabas spoke up on Saul's behalf. Soon Barnabas and Saul were traveling together, sharing the good news of Jesus Christ. It was on one of those trips that scripture stopped referring to Saul as Saul and moved to calling him Paul. This change in usage of his Greek name may coincide with his move to prioritize reaching the Gentile community for Jesus.

Paul is most known for his missionary journeys, taking the testimony of a resurrected Jesus to the Gentiles, most often referred to as the greatest missionary ever. He is credited with writing a significant part of the New Testament with his letters to the different churches he planted. He was beaten, imprisoned, and shipwrecked during his ministry adventures, with several attempts made on his life. He stayed the course of his calling and spoke first to Jews and then to Gentiles, anywhere he went, whether as a free man or as a prisoner.

LESSON 1
REDEMPTION: HOW TO GET UNSTUCK

Introduction: Do you feel stuck? Is life not unfolding the way you wanted or hoped? Life is filled with failures, hardships, and defeats that take their toll on your inner being; they grind you down. No one is exempt from these difficulties. A person's pedigree, education, upbringing, or connection with people of influence cannot prevent difficulties from happening. As my niece, a recent university graduate, says, "Adulting is hard!"

Setbacks may come with great loss. That loss could be financial, personal, professional, or worse yet, all three at once. Some of us tend to approach setbacks in one of two ways. Some will use the setback as a motivator to improve, change, grow, and then move forward. Still others allow the setback to weigh them down—physically, emotionally, spiritually, and mentally. The setback could actually break a person, causing them to give up and then get stuck.

There are myriad resources for those who find motivation in their setbacks. You may seek advice from self-help books, podcasts, blogs, or seek out mentors and coaches. You plan a way forward and begin the journey renewed and energized.

But what about those who feel crushed, who feel their life is over, who have lost hope? You cannot gain motivation from friends, family, self-help books, or coaches and mentors. Your defeat seems final and irrevocable. Whatever resiliency you possessed has been completely drained from you. You are done!

Unfortunately, many of this latter group try self-medicating with alcohol and drugs; others will choose other self-destructive behaviors. All that is accomplished is a continued slide to desolate hopelessness. Unchecked, the ultimate conclusion may be death due to reckless behavior or a conscious decision to end pain through completed suicide.

Have courage and be strong; there is good news! There is a way to get unstuck from the hold that defeat and failure cause. In this week's lesson, you will find that God has made a way through his transformational love to redeem those who are stuck, discouraged, or defeated.

In-depth Study:

Read John 3:16

For God so loved the world that he gave his one and only Son, that whosoever believes in him shall not perish but have eternal life.

God, the creator of humankind, loves us immensely.

What do you love immensely?

How do you protect or help what you love immensely?

Today, we love football, pizza, and our families, yet probably not all in the same way. The English word "love" has too many nuanced meanings to adequately relay the deeper meaning of God's love we see in scripture.

What does *love* mean in John 3:16? The New Testament Greek uses two different words that, in English Bibles, are translated as 'love'. The first is *philos*, which is a brotherly love; Philadelphia has its root in *philos*, which is why we call Philadelphia the city of brotherly love. The second Greek word used is *agapos*, which is a self-sacrificing love. Whenever New Testament scriptures refer to God's love, it is *agapos*, which is used in the above passage. God so self-sacrificingly loved the world that he gave his only Son, Jesus. Jesus, the baby in the manger whom we celebrate at Christmas, is the man who died on a cross as the flawless sacrifice to pay for our sins. All that is required of us is to believe...to accept this unmerited gift.

Read Romans 3:23-24 (NASB) ... for all have sinned and fall short of the glory of God, being justified as a gift by his grace through the redemption which is in Christ Jesus.

Read Romans 6:22-23 But now that you have been set free from sin ... the benefit you reap is eternal life. For the wages of sin is death, but the gift of God is eternal life in Christ Jesus our Lord.

In these biblical passages, as in the John passage, we realize God sees our failures and mistakes, and is making a way for us that is both God's mercy and grace coming through. *Mercy* is God's compassion coming out. God is emotionally moved by those who are hurt, broken, and miserable, those who fail, those who cannot help themselves. *Grace* is God's love in action, forgiving the guilty of their debt by providing a substitute payment, a redeemer. Since we are all guilty of something, God sent Jesus (redeemer), the perfect sacrifice, to pay our deserved wages, that is, death. Jesus died for you and me that we may have eternal life.

Even with this awesome gift of redemption, we have a responsibility to respond to it. We must choose to believe or not. If we believe and accept the gift, we are promised eternal life. Freedom comes to those who receive this undeserved gift from God. In church terms, this is called *salvation*. We are saved from what we deserved, which is eternal separation from God.

Describe a time when you were offered a discount or free gift for participating in an event or promotional.

Did you accept the gift or walk away from it?   Why?

In today's world, we are bombarded with offers of "free" things only to find there is a catch. The wireless company I use offered a new phone "on them" with a trade-in of a qualifying phone. Realizing my phone was nearing disqualification due to its age, my husband and I went in to get the "free" upgrade. As it turned out, the buyback amount was $10 short of the cost of the new phone. A bit annoying, but it was the newest and best phone on the market on that day, and ten dollars for a brand new phone was not that much. The new phones were brought out, our data was all downloaded, and it's time to wrap up the sale. I reached into my wallet to pull out a $20 bill to pay for our "free phones" to find out if I paid cash, the offer was void. We were required to extend our contract for thirty-six months, paying off the twenty dollars at 83 cents a month. Now I am miffed! I believe they lied in their advertising, the old "bait and switch" ploy. To stop the transaction at this point was too painful to even consider. We left the store with new phones, an extended 36-month contract, and a bad opinion regarding this company's practices.

Share an instance when you got an offer that did not live up to the advertisement.

Describe your reactions and feelings.

How has your example tempered your receptiveness to God's offer of unmerited grace from sin, where the only "catch" is to believe?

Application:

Are you held captive by your failures and mistakes? Paul in his letter to the Romans called this "being slaves to sin" (Romans 6:6). Do you feel there is no way to get your life back on track? Do you feel that no one can forgive you for these failures, not even God? God wants to take all that you are (to include mistakes and failures) and make you new! He wants to redeem you... to redeem you from your slavery to sin, to redeem you to a new life of freedom in Jesus.

What is so awful in your life that you do not believe God can forgive you?

List the solutions you attempted to gain redemption/forgiveness from your failure (s)?

How did they help or hinder your healing?

If you have never accepted God's free gift of redemption through his only Son, Jesus, you can do so today. It does not require being a member of a church in good standing. It does not require you to be baptized. It does not require you to clean up your life first. (Though all of those things may follow in the future.) God offers this gift freely and all that is required is to "...declare with your mouth, 'Jesus is Lord,' and believe in your heart that God raised him from the dead, *you will be saved*" (Romans 10:9). Simple and straightforward. You can do this by saying this prayer and truly mean it.

Prayer:

God, I am really messed up, I have failed (sinned against) you. I have no power within myself to fix all that is broken in my life, You know I have tried. I believe you sent your son, Jesus, to earth to pay my debt. I believe he died on a cross and was in the grave for three days, and on the third day you raised him from the dead. I admit I do not understand all of this, but I believe you can do what you say, and I accept this free gift and receive your promise of eternal life. Thank you for sending your son to erase my debt, help me to grow in my new faith this day and every day, in Jesus' name, Amen.

Congratulations on joining the family of God! Like all families we have our favorites and whisper about the eccentric ones, but we have in common praying a prayer similar to the one you just prayed. We all started our life of freedom in God and enjoy the promise of eternal life by accepting God's free gift.

Nothing *magical* happens because you prayed the above prayer; there are still consequences for mistakes, failures, and sin. But like God said to Paul, "My grace is sufficient" (2 Corinthians 12:9). Now you are not alone in your journey. Now you have the mighty living God in your heart and as your guide. God will put in your pathway other believers who are a little further in their redeemed journey to support you, mentor you, and guide you as you grow in your faith. A group Bible study is a good place to start because you will have others working through the same materials and have many of the same questions you do. The writer of the book of Hebrews encouraged Christians, "And let us consider how to stir up one another to love and good works, not neglecting to meet together, as is the habit of some, but encouraging one another..." (Hebrews 10:24-25 ESV). The old adage that "there is strength in numbers" is true in our walk in the faith. Yes, God is enough; however, God designed us, from the beginning, as relational beings. We are spiritually stronger when we surround ourselves with Christian friends, coaches, and mentors.

In the business world, much has been written regarding life coaches and accountability partners. Christians would be wise to take a page or two out of that playbook to ensure we stay focused on God and use his word to guide us. Just because we are redeemed does not mean we will no longer be tempted to do sinful things. Having other Christians investing in us and walking alongside us is another layer of protection from all the ungodly temptations the world has to offer.

Read Ecclesiastes 4:9-12 Two are better than one, because they have a good return for their labor: If either of them falls down, one can help the other up. But pity anyone who falls and has no one to help them up. Also, if two lie down together, they will keep warm. But how can one keep warm alone? Though one may be overpowered, two can defend themselves. A cord of three strands is not quickly broken.

"A cord of three strands is not quickly broken" is often used in marriage ceremonies. Marriages made up of husband, wife, and God are stronger than just the husband and wife alone. Finding a Christian friend to walk with you on your journey with God is imperative to growing in the faith and staying on the right path. As Christians, walking with other Christians and God makes a formidable force against all the world throws at us.

If you are a brand-new Christian, list a few Christian friends or acquaintances you know who could possibly be your accountability partner, prayer partner, or mentor as you continue your life in Jesus, and include their contact information.

| Name: |
| Contact Info: |

| Name: |
| Contact Info: |

| Name: |
| Contact Info: |

For those who have just made a profession of faith, give these contacts a call this next week and share with them your "profession of faith" accepting God's free gift of eternal life through Jesus. Ask them if they would be willing to guide you for this season in your life. Do not be discouraged if some are not available. "No" is as much a holy word as "yes," and you should want those people whom God is calling to walk this journey with you. Not everyone we ask is God's person for us at a particular time. Do not be discouraged; ask someone else if you get a "no" to your request.

When you meet with your mentor, let them know what you want from the relationship. It could be an accountability partner who will check on you regularly to ensure you are not slipping back into old habits. It could be a prayer partner with whom you meet regularly to pray for specific challenges you face. It could be someone with whom you want to enter into a Bible study. Or maybe you are not sure where to start and need a guide as you begin your journey as a Christian. It is important that you and your friend are on the same page and are talking or meeting regularly.

But wait! Maybe you are reading this and you are asking, what about me? I've been a Christian for many years. That is wonderful, your redemption is secure, and much of the above lesson should be a reminder of how truly blessed you have been, knowing your eternal destination is guaranteed. Hopefully, this chapter has brought to mind some of those early mentors and prayer partners you had. Remember to give thanks for those who walked beside you and perhaps send them a message of gratitude. List those early mentors and prayer partners above. Also consider becoming a mentor or prayer partner for a new Christian you know. Have you offered yourself as a mentor or accountability partner for others, or have you fallen into a routine that is automatic without "iron sharpening iron" (Proverbs 27:17). Maybe your prayer should be as follows:

Prayer:

Lord, I have had the privilege to walk with you for many years. Some days I was more faithful than others. Sometimes I let my busyness keep me from studying your word, spending time in prayer, or sharing my journey with others. I am reminded of the Christians who came along side of me early in my walk to encourage and strengthen me. I gave them permission to call me out when I failed to seek you daily. Thank you for putting those Christians in my life when I needed them. Help me to continue to seek out mentors and coaches for my continued growth, as well as, making myself available to those who are seeking you and are new in faith. Guide my steps that I will continue to be a witness for you. Amen.

Closing:

Failure and disappointment are not the words that define you in God's eyes. He sees you as one of his lost children and offers redemption. Once he redeems you, he desires to restore and recycle those failures and disappointments into life lessons that will help you move forward. He desires to repurpose you to his will in a way that you are useful in his kingdom from this day forward. Rejoice! You are a new creature in Jesus! You are a child of God!

Prayer:

Thank you, God, for your continual redeeming love. Help me find a Christian friend who can help me grow in my faith. Help me to find the right person to keep me from falling back into old habits, attitudes, and actions. Guide me now and every day that I may be used to glorify your name. In the saving name of Jesus, Amen.

NOTE PAGE

LESSON 2
REDEEMED: GETTING UNSTUCK V2.0

Introduction: Once you become a Christian, many things change in your life. The newfound faith and redemption have changed your life on earth and for eternity. But it is not always easy to move from your old sinful self to a new life in Jesus. Sometimes you become stuck again.

Friends and family may be skeptical of your new life or actually mock you for it. They "know" you; they have experienced you in your old life. Maybe you have hurt them through your old attitude and behaviors. How many times have you told them you had changed, only to take advantage of them in some way? They do not believe you have changed, and they are not supportive of the direction you want to go.

It is both unsettling and scary when those you are closest to are not convinced. In some scenarios, they even do all they can to bring you back to your old life. "You are not as fun sober!" "What do you mean, you won't have sex with me?" You have become a goodie-two-shoes and a stick-in-the-mud. They laugh at you; they criticize. Many will begin to exclude you from their lives. You are tempted to go back to some of your old habits and old behaviors. You want to be accepted by people who have been important in your life. But you no longer feel good about that life anymore. You are stuck in a no-man's land, and it is uncomfortable and maybe unbearable.

If you have accepted, in faith, the free gift God offered through his son Jesus, then your eternity is secured in heaven when you depart this earthly home (John 3:16). Even though you are redeemed, you may find yourself failing in your actions and thoughts. You question how real your redemption could be since you have failed so miserably. Let scripture be clear, God is enough! God tells Paul that "My grace is sufficient for you, for my power is made perfect in weakness" (2 Corinthians 12:9). Paul had an issue. Scripture does not reveal what it was, but Paul called it a "thorn in his flesh" (2 Corinthians 12:7). Paul's point was that even though he prayed for this "thorn" to be removed on several occasions, God's answer was, I am enough! I am with you and will get you through it.

In-depth Study:

Even though we know in our hearts that God is enough, in our heads we get easily confused and misled by all the world throws at us. Our relationship with God tends to follow a cycle. We see it with the people of Israel in the Old Testament, especially in the book of Judges. From the beginning, God has loved us. God has compassion for how miserable our lives become when we seek our own desires versus seeking his way.

God's compassion for us is his *love* coming out. This leads to his plan for people like us, which we see as his *mercy*. The plan from the beginning was a blood sacrifice. It started in the Garden of Eden after Adam and Eve ate the fruit from the one tree in the garden that was prohibited (Genesis 1–3). Adam and Eve realized they were naked and were afraid (before the television show). They were ashamed to be seen by God. Therefore, God sacrificed some animals so Adam and Eve could be clothed in something more substantial than their sewn fig leaves.

The people of Israel, God's chosen people, were given God's law through Moses, which included many sacrifices that were required (not all were animals; some were grain, oil, or incense). Finally, God sent Jesus to earth in the form of a human baby who would ultimately die on a cross for all of our sins (past, present, and future). When Jesus died on the cross, once for all (Romans 6:10), we see God's *grace* at work. As we learned in Lesson 1, our only requirement is to repent and believe, that is, to accept God's gift, which allows for our *redemption*. Once we are redeemed, we become Christians and disciples of Jesus and his teachings. The Bible provides instructions on living in harmony with God. The more we read and learn from God's word, the more we realize that God is calling us into *obedient service*. Obedient service can mean as little as keeping the 10 commandments (Exodus 20:1–17) or as much as becoming a pastor or missionary to teach and preach about Jesus. For most of us, it is something in the middle. We grow in understanding and knowledge of God's word, and that understanding and knowledge move us into action, serving God and others. This is the "sweet spot" in our faith journey, when we are grounded and growing in faith, knowledge, and understanding, and then putting into action the love, mercy, and grace we have received to help others.

Unfortunately, as fallible humans, we get cocky and believe all the good we are doing is in our own strength, or we get lazy. We begin to limit our time in worship and personal Bible study, or we fall to the temptations of this world. Whatever the reason, we fail to be all God wants us to be. This should last for a short time, but sometimes our fall is bigger and longer. It is not until we get called out by another Christian or by those non-Christians who are watching our hypocrisy that we realize we are back in the misery of failure in our relationship with God. And God once again has compassion for us and leads us back to himself. The diagram below attempts to show visually what was discussed above.

Serve God and others
When We Fail
God has compassion for our misery
God Call Us to Obedient Service
God's love
God's Transformational Love and Grace
God creates plan to redeem us
We become Jesus' disciples
God's Mercy
God's Redemption
God's Grace
God sends Jesus as our redeemer
We repent and believe

How did you go from an evil doer and sinner to a redeemed disciple of Jesus?

What baggage do you carry from your old life without God that weighs you down today?

Who or what has helped you jettison this old baggage?

Read Romans 12:1-2 Therefore, I urge you, brothers and sisters, in view of God's mercy, to offer your bodies as a living sacrifice, holy and pleasing to God—this is your true and proper worship. 2 Do not conform to the pattern of this world, but be transformed by the renewing of your mind. Then you will be able to test and approve what God's will is—his good, pleasing, and perfect will.

Paul was calling the Christians in the Roman church to offer themselves as "living sacrifices, holy and pleasing to God" (Romans 12:1). Under the Old Testament covenant, the people of Israel were responsible for offering sacrifices to God at different times of the year and for different atonements when they had broken God's law as given through Moses. Paul argues that, in Christ, we are no longer under the burden of the "Law of Moses" because Jesus had become the once and for all sacrifice for our sins (Romans 6:10). Therefore, sacrifice in the tradition of the Old Testament is no longer required; however, this new relationship with God, the Father, through Jesus, his son does require us to live holy and obedient lives.

What does a life lived "holy and pleasing to God" look like for you?

Who would you say would be an example of a life lived holy and pleasing to God? Why?

Paul goes on to tell us in Romans 12:2 how we accomplish this holy living when he states it in both negative and positive ways. He says, "Do not be conformed, any longer to the pattern of the world." Conformity is demanded more and more in our society. No longer can Christians keep their heads down and their mouths shut regarding behaviors condemned in scripture but acceptable in society. It is no longer acceptable to disagree with others, for the disagreement is no longer about an issue, but it is a direct attack on another's personhood. For some, the only acceptable stance is that you not only agree with them but must openly advocate their positions. To do less is to be vilified by society. That is conforming to this world.

Up until junior high, I felt I was fairly independent in my style and beliefs. Once I entered 7th grade, the last thing I wanted to be was different. I began to be conscious of what clothes I wore, how I spoke, and even what I ate because it was all under a microscope. What and who was "in" depended on the "popular" teens, of which I was not one. It was a nerve-racking time in my life. To survive junior and senior high, conformity was a must. It made the time at school more tolerable, but it was disingenuous and, quite frankly, miserable for me sometimes.

As Christians, we need to understand up front and early *in* our walk that being people of faith makes us different. Though we must be in the world, we should not be *of* the world. (This is not a scripture quote but a concept we see throughout scripture.) We must sound different from the world; we must act differently from the world. Paul gives us the how to be different in his positive description of how to embrace holy living. Paul tells us we need to "be transformed by the renewing of our minds."

List the area(s) in your life that you conform to the world's standard.

The only way we can combat all of what the world is presenting, whether in the news, on television, in theaters or on social media, is to be well grounded in God's word. Studying God's word as an individual or in small groups is imperative to "renewing our minds." The old computer programmer's adage of "junk in, junk out" holds true with Christians. If all we see and hear is what the world projects, it becomes easy to accept as normal some clearly evil/sinful behaviors. I believe this started years ago with the reality show *Survivor.* To win the money at the end, contestants lied, cheated, back stabbed, and sabotaged their fellow contestants. The more vicious the betrayals the more votes they got from the viewers. The show got more popular as the viciousness of competition rose.

Name other popular shows/commercials that encourage us to violate God's standards?

Describe what you see as the most frequent violations of God's standards in shows and commercials?

Name shows on television or live stream that reflects God's values.

Isaiah, an Old Testament prophet, wrote "Woe to those who call evil good, and good evil; Who put darkness for light, and light for darkness; Who put bitter for sweet, and sweet for bitter" (Isaiah 5:20). That is what is happening all around us. The world is selling lies, and if we do not stay grounded in God's word, allowing God to renew our hearts and minds every day, we too can fall to the lies.

Application:

Even Paul the Apostle struggled to do God's will perfectly all the time. "For I do not do the good I want, but I do the very evil I do not want" (Romans 7:19). Yet look how God used him to spread the Good News of the Gospel of Jesus around the known world. He too failed God and the church; yet God continued to renew and transform him into a servant who did marvelous work for God's kingdom. The reason he was used so mightily by God is that he refused to stay in his sinful/disobedient status. He was always prepared to repent and believe, accept God's pardon, and move forward.

What has kept you stuck since becoming a Christian?

How has conforming to the world contributed to you being stuck?

What steps can you take to move away from the "evil you do not want to do?"

Closing:

Have you asked for God's forgiveness and his help to be transformed? If you have not, here is a simple prayer you can recite.

Prayer: Holy God, as King David prayed, "Against you, you only, have I sinned and done evil in your sight; so you are right in your verdict and justified when you judge..." (Psalm 51:4). O Lord, help me to follow your teachings, help me to walk in your ways. Help me to be transformed by your holy word. Provide in my heart a desire to seek knowledge and understanding of your standards so I may stand up against the evil that attacks my senses every waking moment. Place your hedge of protection around my heart and mind that I may stay focused on you and not be easily persuaded to seek the world's ways that bring hardship and misery. Thank you for being so ready to heal my heart when I return to you and your ways. I pray in Jesus' name, amen.

NOTE PAGE

LESSON 3
RESTORATION: COMES WITH REPENTANCE

Introduction: After years of moving across the country and to Europe as a military family, my husband and I found ourselves in Colorado Springs, Colorado, in need of some new living room furniture. We are not fans of particle board furniture, and we were disappointed that every couch and loveseat we looked at did not fit my five-foot frame. In every furniture showroom, I felt like Edith Ann, the character Lily Tomlin played on *Rowan & Martin's Laugh-In* in the late sixties, where she played a little girl sitting in a giant rocking chair. My legs were not long enough to even bend at the knee, so they stuck straight out. New furniture was being built to accommodate the ever-growing girth of Americans, not a petite woman. We turned to antique furniture.

Shopping around in antique stores for restored couches, I finally found one. It was beautiful, and I could sit in it with my feet touching the floor without slouching. I approached the owner, but he quite emphatically said, "Not for Sale!" He had his reasons, but I needed something in my living room that would work for me. Finally, having pity on this persistent woman, he took us across the street to an old railroad storage building. We climbed up the metal ladder attached to the loading dock. Once inside the cramped and dusty space, the owner presented two 1940s circa settees. The wood was painted white, and the upholstery was a champagne color with 2-inch green stripes. The upholstery was worn, with many of the buttons missing on the cushions; in a word, they were hideous. Yet, I could sit in one comfortably, and they could be restored.

We purchased the set and used them, as ugly as they were, for a couple more moves before landing in North Carolina for an assignment. It was time to have the settees restored. A gentleman who owned a furniture restoration business came to our home but made no guarantees about what he could do. I wanted to dump the paint and go back to natural wood and then upholster them in something that fit the eclectic antique furniture we already owned. Because of the paint, the shop owner could not tell if the wood was of a high enough quality to stain. Once the furniture was stripped of its paint, the restorer not only found beautiful maple wood, but also that the settees had inlaid designs as well, which the paint had hidden. When he was finished restoring the settees, we had beautiful furniture that complemented our other pieces and a story about what can be accomplished with a master at restoration.

Today's lesson will look at how God is truly the master at restoring his people, making us better than we were before. He removes the ugliness of our sinful living and restores us to the beautiful, useful beings he created us to be. I was thankful to find a master who could restore my settees; yet I'm overjoyed with thankfulness to have found God, **the Master Restorer of people!**

In-Depth Study:

King David was the second king of Israel. Before Israel demanded a king, the priest was the spiritual leader of the twelve tribes. However, the priest at the time, Samuel, had wicked sons who did evil in the sight of God. The elders approached Samuel with the request for a king, like all the nations around them had. Up to this point, God had led the people through his appointed priests. God was their protector, guardian, King above all kings; yet he was not flesh and blood. He was not present in the same ways as the kings of the nations around them were. They wanted to look like their neighbors (*conformity*). God gave them Saul. Unfortunately, though Saul's reign started out well, he became disobedient to God's commands and did evil in God's sight. God grieved that he had made Saul king over Israel (1 Samuel 1–15). While Saul was still alive, God withdrew his blessing on him as king and had Samuel anoint David as king. As one can imagine, there was strife, for Saul refused to give up the kingship and made attempts on David's life. Saul eventually dies by his own hand after being critically wounded by the Philistine archers (1 Samuel 31).

In Acts 13, while speaking in the synagogue at Antioch, Paul the Apostle gave a quick summary of the people of Israel's history. Paul says, "And when [God] removed [Saul], he raised up unto them David to be their king; to whom also he gave this testimony, and said, I have found David the son of Jesse, *a man after mine own heart*, which shall fulfil my will" (Acts 13:22-23). I can think of no other greater words God could use to describe a disciple than to say he was "a person after his own heart." And yet, David had weaknesses and failures that he had to confront. The most notable failure is when he lusted after another man's wife.

Read 2 Samuel 11 (NASB) Then it happened in the spring, at the time when kings go out to battle, that David sent Joab and his servants with him and all Israel, and they brought destruction on the sons of Ammon and besieged Rabbah. But David stayed in Jerusalem. 2 Now at evening time, David got up from his bed and walked around on the roof of the king's house, and from the roof he saw a woman bathing; and the woman was very beautiful in appearance. 3 So David sent servants and inquired about the woman. And someone said, "Is this not Bathsheba, the daughter of Eliam, the wife of Uriah the Hittite?" 4 Then David sent messengers and had her brought, and when she came to him, he slept with her; and when she had purified herself from her uncleanness, she returned to her house. 5 But the woman conceived; so she sent word and informed David, and said, "I am pregnant." 6 Then David sent word to Joab: "Send me Uriah the Hittite." So Joab sent Uriah to David. 7 When Uriah came to him, David asked about Joab's well-being and that of the people, and the condition of the war. 8 Then David said to Uriah, "Go down to your house, and wash your feet." So Uriah left the king's house, and a gift from the king was sent after him. 9 But Uriah slept at the door of the king's house with all the servants of his lord, and did not go down to his house. 10 Now, when they informed David, saying, "Uriah did not go down to his house," David said to Uriah, "Did you not come from a journey? Why did you not go down to your house?" 11 And Uriah said to David, "The ark and Israel and Judah are staying in temporary shelters, and my lord Joab and the servants of my lord are camping in the open field. Should I then go to my house to eat and drink and to sleep with my wife? By your life and the life of your soul, I will not do this thing." 12 Then David said to Uriah, "Stay here today also, and tomorrow I will let you go back." So Uriah remained in Jerusalem that day and the day after. 13 Now David summoned Uriah, and he ate and drank in his presence, and he made Uriah drunk; and in the evening, Uriah went out to lie on his bed with his lord's servants, and he still did not go down to his house. 14 So in the morning, David wrote a letter to Joab and sent it by the hand of Uriah. 15 He had written in the letter the following: "Station Uriah on the front line of the fiercest battle and pull back from him, so that he may be struck and killed." 16 So it was as Joab kept watch on the city, that he stationed Uriah at the place where he knew there were valiant men. 17 And the men of the city went out and fought against Joab, and some of the people among David's servants fell; and Uriah the Hittite also died. 18 Then Joab sent a messenger and reported to David all the events of the war. 19 He ordered the messenger, saying, "When you have finished telling all the events of the war to the king. 20 then it shall be that if the king's wrath rises and he says to you, 'Why did you move against the city to fight? Did you not know that they would shoot from the wall? 21 Who struck Abimelech, the son of Jerubbesheth? Did a woman not throw an upper millstone on him from the wall so that he died at Thebez? Why did you move against the wall?'—then you shall say, 'Your servant Uriah the Hittite also died.'" 22 So the messenger departed and came and reported to David everything that Joab had sent him to tell. 23 The messenger said to David, "The men prevailed against us and came out against us in the field, but we pressed them as far as the entrance of the gate. 24 Also, the archers shot at your servants from the wall; so some of the king's servants died, and your servant Uriah the Hittite also died." 25 Then David said to the messenger, "This is what you shall say to Joab: 'Do not let this thing displease you, for the sword devours one as well as another; fight with determination against the city and overthrow it'; and thereby encourage him." 26 Now when Uriah's wife heard that her husband Uriah was dead, she mourned for her husband. 27 When the time of mourning was over, David sent servants and had her brought to his house, and she became his wife; then she bore him a son. But the thing that David had done was evil in the sight of the Lord.

Much happens in this passage. It starts with the king choosing not to accompany his army into battle. There is no reason given, but it is clear that this was unusual behavior for David or any king. Because David was not where he should have been, he finds himself restless, that is, "got up from his bed and walked around on the roof of the king's house" (2 Samuel 11:2, NASB).

While looking out from the rooftop, he saw a beautiful woman bathing. Rather than going back to his many wives, he lusted after this woman and sent messengers to find her. Even after being told she was Uriah's wife, he had her brought to him in the palace. He then committed adultery with her. The plot thickened as she contacted him later with the news that she was pregnant.

Bathsheba's husband, Uriah the Hittite, was with the army fighting the Ammonites; he was also one of David's thirty mighty men (1 Chronicles 11:41). David's treachery continued. He sent word to his army commander to send Uriah back to Jerusalem. Under the pretense of receiving a report from the field, David asked a myriad of questions. When Uriah finished the report, David sent Uriah to his home. David's thought was that Uriah would have sex with his wife; later, when he found out she was pregnant, he would assume the child was his. However, Uriah does not go home, nor does he have sex with his wife. Thus, unbeknown to Uriah, he foiled David's attempt to cover up his sin. However, David would not be thwarted in his cover-up. He told Uriah to stay another night, got him drunk, and sent him home, believing that he would have sex with his wife; Uriah did not.

David was frustrated at every turn by Uriah's dedication to the troops in the field, David penned orders for Uriah to take back to the commander of the army. Uriah had no idea what the orders were and faithfully delivered the king's message. David's order was "Station Uriah on the front line of the fiercest battle and pull back from him, so that he may be struck and killed." (2 Samuel 11:15, NASB). Uriah was killed, and David married Bathsheba, Uriah's wife.

List the sins David committed in this passage.

Why do you think David believed he could do these things without consequences?

Read 2 Samuel 12 (ESV) And the Lord sent Nathan to David. He came to him and said to him, "There were two men in a certain city, the one rich and the other poor. 2 The rich man had very many flocks and herds, 3 but the poor man had nothing but one little ewe lamb, which he had bought. And he brought it up, and it grew up with him and with his children. It used to eat of his morsel and drink from his cup and lie in his arms, and it was like a daughter to him. 4 Now there came a traveler to the rich man, and he was unwilling to take one of his own flock or herd to prepare for the guest who had come to him, but he took the poor man's lamb and prepared it for the man who had come to him." 5 Then David's anger was greatly kindled against the man, and he said to Nathan, "As the Lord lives, the man who has done this deserves to die, 6 and he shall restore the lamb fourfold, because he did this thing, and because he had no pity." 7 Nathan said to David, "You are the man! Thus says the Lord, the God of Israel, 'I anointed you king over Israel, and I delivered you out of the hand of Saul. 8 And I gave you your master's house and your master's wives into your arms and gave you the house of Israel and of Judah. And if this were too little, I would add to you as much more. 9 Why have you despised the word of the Lord, to do what is evil in his sight? You have struck down Uriah the Hittite with the sword and have taken his wife to be your wife and have killed him with the sword of the Ammonites. 10 Now therefore the sword shall never depart from your house, because you have despised me and have taken the wife of Uriah the Hittite to be your wife.' 11 Thus says the Lord, 'Behold, I will raise up evil against you out of your own house. And I will take your wives before your eyes and give them to your neighbor, and he shall lie with your wives in the sight of this sun. 12 For you did it secretly, but I will do this thing before all Israel and before the sun.'" 13 David said to Nathan, "I have sinned against the Lord." And Nathan said to David, "The Lord also has put away your sin; you shall not die. 14 Nevertheless, because by this deed you have utterly scorned the Lord, the child who is born to you shall die." 15 Then Nathan went to his house. And the Lord afflicted the child that Uriah's wife bore to David, and he became sick. 16 David therefore sought God on behalf of the child. And David fasted and went in and lay all night on the ground. 17 And the elders of his house stood beside him, to raise him from the ground, but he would not, nor did he eat food with them. 18 On the seventh day, the child died. And the servants of David were afraid to tell him that the child was dead, for they said, "Behold, while the child was yet alive, we spoke to him, and he did not listen to us. How then can we say to him that the child is dead? He may do himself some harm." 19 But when David saw that his servants were whispering together, David understood that the child was dead. And David said to his servants, "Is the child dead?" They said, "He is dead." 20 Then David arose from the earth and washed and anointed himself and changed his clothes. And he went into the house of the Lord and worshiped. He then went to his own house. And when he asked, they set food before him, and he ate. 21 Then his servants said to him, "What is this thing that you have done? You fasted and wept for the child while he was alive, but when the child died, you arose and ate food." 22 He said, "While the child was still alive, I fasted and wept, for I said, 'Who knows whether the Lord will be gracious to me, that the child may live?' 23 But now he is dead. Why should I fast? Can I bring him back again? I shall go to him, but he will not return to me." 24 Then David comforted his wife, Bathsheba, and went in to her and lay with her, and she bore a son, and he called his name Solomon. And the Lord loved him 25 and sent a message by Nathan the prophet. So he called his name Jedidiah, because of the Lord. 26 Now Joab fought against Rabbah of the Ammonites and took the royal city. 27 And Joab sent messengers to David and said, "I have fought against Rabbah; moreover, I have taken the city of waters. 28 Now then, gather the rest of the people together and encamp against the city and take it, lest I take the city and it be called by my name." 29 So David gathered all the people together and went to Rabbah and fought against it and took it. 30 And he took the crown of their king from his head. The weight of it was a talent of gold, and in it was a precious stone, and it was placed on David's head. And he brought out the spoil of the city, a very great amount. 31 And he brought out the people who were in it and set them to labor with saws and iron picks and iron axes and made them toil at the brick kilns. And thus he did to all the cities of the Ammonites. Then David and all the people returned to Jerusalem.

List the similarities between Nathan's story to David and what David did in chapter 11.

What was David's reaction to Nathan's story?

Wow! David shirked his duty as the king, lusted after a woman who was the wife of one of his closest warriors, impregnated her, tried to cover it up, and when that failed, ordered the woman's husband to be murdered in battle, then took her as his wife. Not the behavior a reasonable person would expect from "a man after God's own heart."

Nathan, a prophet, was sent by God to confront King David. Nathan told David a story of injustice, and scripture tells us David "burned with anger." Nathan said to him, "You are the man!"

Application:

To say God was not pleased with David is a monumental understatement. There are consequences for all the sin that takes place in 2 Samuel 11. Nathan is called on by God to outline the consequences David will face. The consequences for his sin – God told David through Nathan that he would face combat (the sword) the rest of his days, and that out of his own household, calamity would come. On top of that, the child born from this adulterous affair would become ill and die after 7 days. Yet, even with all this, God still used David to do his will and bring glory to his holy name because David first repented before God and lived a life of faith and devotion. David did indeed become "a man after God's own heart." The kicker in the story is that Bathsheba became the mother of Solomon, David's son who would become king and build the Temple of the Lord in Jerusalem, something David longed to do, but God would not allow (1 Chronicles 17:1-15, 22:6-10)

Remember in Lesson 1, we looked at the passage in Romans 3:23, "...for all have sinned and fallen short of the glory of God." Sin always has consequences. Sin is doing evil in God's eyes

List the consequences for David's sins as outlined by Nathan.

What did David deserve based on the Mosaic Law?

What did God spare David from?

What evil have you done in God's sight? (Psalm 51:4)

What did you do to cover up or hide your sin?

What were the consequences of your sin?

What did you learn from this experience?

How do you recognize and avoid such failures in the future?

Who became your Nathan during this situation?

Psalm 51 was written by David after Nathan had confronted him about his actions as described in 2 Samuel 11-12. David came face to face with the fact that he truly had done evil in the sight of God, and this psalm is his confession, repentance, lament, and promise all rolled into a song.

Read Psalm 51 Have mercy on me, O God, according to your unfailing love; according to your great compassion blot out my transgressions. 2 Wash away all my iniquity and cleanse me from my sin. 3 For I know my transgressions and my sin is always before me. 4 Against you, you only, have I sinned and done what is evil in your sight; so you are right in your verdict and justified when you judge. 5 Surely I was sinful at birth, sinful from the time my mother conceived me. 6 Yet you desired faithfulness even in the womb; you taught me wisdom in that secret place. 7 Cleanse me with hyssop, and I will be clean; wash me, and I will be whiter than snow. 8 Let me hear joy and gladness; let the bones you have crushed rejoice. 9 Hide your face from my sins and blot out all my iniquity. 10 Create in me a pure heart, O God, and renew a steadfast spirit within me. 11 Do not cast me from your presence or take your Holy Spirit from me. 12 Restore to me the joy of your salvation and grant me a willing spirit, to sustain me. 13 Then I will teach transgressors your ways, so that sinners will turn back to you. 14 Deliver me from the guilt of bloodshed, O God, you who are God my Savior, and my tongue will sing of your righteousness. 15 Open my lips, Lord, and my mouth will declare your praise. 16 You do not delight in sacrifice, or I would bring it; you do not take pleasure in burnt offerings. 17 My sacrifice, O God, is a broken spirit; a broken and contrite heart you, God, will not despise. 18 May it please you to prosper Zion, to build up the walls of Jerusalem. 19 Then you will delight in the sacrifices of the righteous, in burnt offerings offered whole; then bulls will be offered on your altar.

David admitted his guilt and sin. He had experienced first-hand what it was like not being in favor with God. David yearned for the relationship to be restored.

What does David ask of God in Psalm 51?

Though you may not be guilty of all that David did in 2 Samuel 11, when you have sinned, it is first and foremost against God. The only way to be restored is to repent and ask God for forgiveness. If you do not seek forgiveness and restoration, you will again become stuck, separated from God and no longer in God's will; you will not be used as an instrument for God's glory.

What did it take for you to approach God in repentance?

How is God using you since he "restored you to the joy of his salvation?"

Closing:

God is not only the great physician, but he is the master at soul restoration. He will not let you get away with sin, even when done in secret. He will bring those sins to the light so you may confess and lament them, seek forgiveness, and offer restitution, moving forward, serving him faithfully. God wants to restore you to be his faithful servant and witness. Come before God with "a contrite heart" and allow him to restore you for his glory. You can do this by praying this simple prayer.

Prayer:

God, the Master Restorer, your word calls me to holy living, yet I sometimes fail. Whether through my pride or disobedience, I make terrible decisions which mar and scar me. I hurt those around me. The unintended negative consequences can sometimes cause death, whether physical or spiritual. Send a Nathan into my life when I sin against you. Call me back to yourself and restore me so that I might again serve you boldly and with your power. May I once again be the person after your own heart. I pray, Amen.

NOTE PAGE

LESSON 4
REPURPOSE: GOD TAKES WHATEVER WE GIVE HIM FOR HIS PURPOSE

Introduction: My high school friend and her husband spend their weekends "picking." They scour garage sales, estate sales, things left on the curb, things discarded. They bring their finds home and begin to repurpose them for sale. They give outdated, yet not antique furniture a new purpose. I marvel at the before and after pictures Beth posts on her Facebook page called "Bloom & Begin Again." Beth and Bob are imaginative and can look beyond the reality of a piece to what can be with a bit of creativity and hard work.

God is that way! He sees beyond our dents, scars, and chips to what we can be for his kingdom. When God finds us discarded by the world as used up, out of touch, shamed, guilty, and going the wrong direction, he sees promise, he sees potential, he sees how he can repurpose us to do great things for him.

In this lesson, we will look at a man who was on the fast track to be a leading member of the Sanhedrin, the most powerful body in the Jewish hierarchy, often called the rulers or the ruling council. A Jew above Jews! A man who had gone to the best rabbinical schools and knew the Law of Moses better than any of his contemporaries. He was pious and a zealous follower of the faith. Let us look at how God took this man and repurposed him to be the greatest Christian missionary the world has known. You guessed it. This lesson is about Saul the Hebrew of Hebrews who became Paul the missionary to the Gentiles..

In-Depth Study:

The book of Acts, also known as the Acts of the Apostles, is the history of the early church after the death and resurrection of Jesus. It begins with the last time the eleven remaining disciples saw Jesus on earth. Jesus instructed the disciples to stay in Jerusalem until the Holy Spirit comes. Peter is central to the first several chapters as he preached, taught, and healed people in and around Jerusalem. But all was not well in the world.

The High Priest with the Pharisees and Sadducees were still unhappy with this movement of people who continued to follow Jesus' teachings even though they had successfully executed Jesus. The religious leaders brought the Apostles and anyone following Jesus' teachings to face the Sanhedrin, the highest ruling body among the Jews. In fact, they were actively hunting down people of "the Way" to dissuade others from following this movement. They arrested those followers, and eventually they stoned those who were caught practicing this "heresy." This is where we get introduced to Saul in scripture.

"Now Stephen, a man full of God's grace and power..." was seized and brought before the Sanhedrin. Stephen spoke with God's power and eventually called the Jewish elite "stiff-necked people." For this declaration and testimony, he was attacked and stoned to death (Acts 6-7). Almost as a footnote, Acts 7:58 mentions that Saul was there.

Read Acts 8:1-3 On that day a great persecution broke out against the church in Jerusalem, and all except the apostles were scattered throughout Judea and Samaria. 2 Godly men buried Stephen and mourned deeply for him. 3 But Saul began to destroy the church. Going from house to house, he dragged off both men and women and put them in prison.

What happens after Stephen's death?

What does Saul do?

Read Acts 9:1-19 Meanwhile, Saul was still breathing out murderous threats against the Lord's disciples. He went to the high priest 2 and asked him for letters to the synagogues in Damascus, so that if he found any there who belonged to the Way, whether men or women, he might take them as prisoners to Jerusalem. 3 As he neared Damascus on his journey, suddenly a light from heaven flashed around him. 4 He fell to the ground and heard a voice say to him, "Saul, Saul, why do you persecute me?" 5 "Who are you, Lord?" Saul asked. "I am Jesus, whom you are persecuting," he replied. 6 "Now get up and go into the city, and you will be told what you must do." 7 The men traveling with Saul stood there speechless; they heard the sound but did not see anyone. 8 Saul got up from the ground, but when he opened his eyes he could see nothing. So they led him by the hand into Damascus. 9 For three days, he was blind and did not eat or drink anything. 10 In Damascus, there was a disciple named Ananias. The Lord called to him in a vision, "Ananias!" "Yes, Lord," he answered. 11 The Lord told him, "Go to the house of Judas on Straight Street and ask for a man from Tarsus named Saul, for he is praying. 12 In a vision he has seen a man named Ananias come and place his hands on him to restore his sight." 13 "Lord," Ananias answered, "I have heard many reports about this man and all the harm he has done to your holy people in Jerusalem. 14 And he has come here with authority from the chief priests to arrest all who call on your name." 15 But the Lord said to Ananias, "Go! This man is my chosen instrument to proclaim my name to the Gentiles and their kings and to the people of Israel. 16 I will show him how much he must suffer for my name." 17 Then Ananias went to the house and entered it. Placing his hands on Saul, he said, "Brother Saul, the Lord Jesus, who appeared to you on the road as you were coming here, has sent me so that you may see again and be filled with the Holy Spirit." 18 Immediately, something like scales fell from Saul's eyes, and he could see again. He got up and was baptized, 19 and after taking some food, he regained his strength. Saul spent several days with the disciples in Damascus.

Did you catch the language used in verses 1-2? "Still breathing out murderous threats..." Saul was all in for destroying the Christian movement and its believers by any means possible. Saul went as far as getting letters authorizing him to arrest anyone in Damascus who was part of "the Way."

And yet, God is about to have an encounter with Saul that changed everything. Literally, Saul saw the light! As if the blinding light was not scary enough, Jesus confronted him, "Saul, Saul, why do you persecute me? I am Jesus, whom you are persecuting." Jesus made it clear he was talking specifically to Saul.

I cannot imagine what was going through Saul's mind. A brilliant light has blinded him, and the voice of Jesus explained that he knows everything Saul has done. There is no place to hide, no room for denials; he was caught with letters in his possession giving him wide latitude to do with Jesus' followers anything he desired. Talk about being caught "red-handed." Rather than ending Saul's life on the spot for all the sinful things he had done, Jesus saw Saul's potential. With Saul's education, zeal, and prominence, God recognized he could repurpose Saul for his mission! Jesus directed Saul to go to Damascus and told him he would be shown what to do.

Saul had an incredible encounter with the risen Jesus. He was blinded and at the mercy of his traveling companions to get him to Damascus.

What thoughts and feelings would flood your heart and mind if you had been Saul on this road?

What would you say in your own defense?

What could be said to Saul's companions who heard a sound but neither saw nor heard what Saul had?

Then the scene moves to the disciple Ananias. Ananias was not too keen at being called to talk with Saul. He was afraid of Saul and his reputation. The disciples knew why Saul was coming to Damascus and were living in fear. Ananias stated his case, but the Lord said, "Go! This man is my chosen instrument to carry my name before the Gentiles and their kings and before the people of Israel" (Acts 9:15).

I do not know about Ananias, but I'd be shaking in my sandals! I would certainly hope I had misunderstood my instructions. I might even try to "slow roll" the inevitable. Yet, Ananias was obedient and served God in this manner. God saw potential in Saul, something that neither Ananias nor anyone else could.

Saul had been fasting and praying for three days when Ananias came to him. Saul received his sight, was baptized, and took food to regain his strength.

What would you say to God who called you to go talk with this persecutor of the church?

Read Acts 9:20-31 (ESV) 20 And immediately he proclaimed Jesus in the synagogues, saying, "He is the Son of God." 21 And all who heard him were amazed and said, "Is not this the man who made havoc in Jerusalem of those who called upon this name? And has he not come here for this purpose, to bring them bound before the chief priests?" 22 But Saul increased all the more in strength, and confounded the Jews who lived in Damascus by proving that Jesus was the Christ. 23 When many days had passed, the Jews plotted to kill him, 24 but their plot became known to Saul. They were watching the gates day and night to kill him, 25 but his disciples took him by night and let him down through an opening in the wall, lowering him in a basket. 26 And when he had come to Jerusalem, he attempted to join the disciples. And they were all afraid of him, for they did not believe that he was a disciple. 27 But Barnabas took him and brought him to the apostles and declared to them how on the road he had seen the Lord, who spoke to him, and how at Damascus he had preached boldly in the name of Jesus. 28 So he went in and out among them at Jerusalem, preaching boldly in the name of the Lord. 29 And he spoke and disputed against the Hellenists. But they were seeking to kill him. 30 And when the brothers learned this, they brought him down to Caesarea and sent him off to Tarsus. 31 So the church throughout all Judea and Galilee and Samaria had peace and was being built up. And walking in the fear of the Lord and in the comfort of the Holy Spirit, it multiplied.

In Saul's early days as a new Christian, he began to preach in the synagogues that Jesus was the Son of God. The reviews of his newfound faith tended to be one of confusion and doubt. The confusion and doubt brought on by the fact that Saul, just days earlier, had the authority to arrest any person who believed in Jesus. How could Saul so radically change, and how did he speak with such power?

As scripture explains, the Jewish leaders were not happy; in fact, they plotted to kill Saul. The situation was so dangerous that Saul had to be lowered in a basket through an opening in the city wall. Many of Saul's early preachings came with his needing to get out of town quickly. God had repurposed Saul from persecutor of Christians to a powerful teacher and preacher for Christ.

An interesting thing happened when Saul arrived in Jerusalem. None of the disciples trusted him to be a brother in Christ. They figured as zealous as Saul had been against Christians this could be a ploy that would lead to additional arrests and stoning. In verse 27, scripture tells us, "But Barnabas took him and brought him to the apostles." Barnabas vouched for Saul's sincerity and gave testimony to his preaching in Damascus. However, the Hellenist Jews plotted to kill Saul, and the brothers of faith moved him again.

Since you turned from your old life to a new life in Christ, who doubts your authenticity in the faith?

Who comes alongside you to vouch for you and your faith?

How does this person (these people) "Stand in the gap" for you with the church members, family, and friends?

We learn in Acts 11 that Barnabas went to Antioch to minister to the church there. Barnabas went to Tarsus to find Saul and took him back to Antioch with him. There, Barnabas and Saul worked together for a year, an opportunity for Barnabas to mentor Saul and to partner in ministry.

In Acts 13, Barnabas and Saul are set apart by God for a special ministry. It is in Acts 13:9 where scriptures stop using Saul's Jewish name and begin using his Roman name Paul; both names he received at birth since his parents were Jewish yet also held Roman citizenship. As led by the Holy Spirit, Barnabas and Paul traveled preaching and teaching wherever they went. God had taken the Hebrew of Hebrews, the zealous persecutor of the early church, and repurposed him to take the good news of Jesus first to the Jews, then to the Gentiles.

Application:

When I was nine years old, I accepted God's free gift of salvation through Jesus. For many reasons, I did not receive much instruction in what it is to be a new creature in Christ. It was not until I was in high school that I realized I needed to live my faith, which meant changes in my life. It was not that I was a troubled youth or a troublemaker; I was just living life as I wanted with no acknowledgment that God might want more of me.

I had a mentor in our youth minister and a pastor who spent many sermons teaching about discipleship and what that entailed. In my naïveté, I decided in my mind that I was going to North Texas State University (NTSU at the time) on a basketball scholarship (or as a walk on) majoring in accounting. I would become a wealthy Certified Public Accountant (CPA) and ensure every child or youth who wanted to go to a Christian camp or conference would have the funds to do so. I'm not sure where this noble dream came from, but it was important to me and I intended to make it a reality.

Someone once said, "If you want me to make God laugh, tell him your plans." I guess God got a big laugh over my dream. I loved basketball, all five feet of me; it was my way to a scholarship and the beginning of my journey to reach my dream as a wealthy CPA. Yet, it was this love of basketball and tearing up my knee that upended my dream. My senior year, I tore my meniscus; after graduation, I had arthroscopic surgery to repair it. This turned out to be more complicated than a simple repair. I started my college career on crutches at the small county college near my home. I never got to NTSU or played basketball for any team. I ended up at a small university across the state line, to which I could commute. Rather than a business degree in accounting, I ended up with a bachelor's degree in education. Then off to seminary.

God repurposed my life, not losing anything I learned along the way, but refocused it in totally different and unimagined ways. I went from dreaming of being a CPA to becoming an Air Force Chaplain (and yes, I was in charge of the chaplain fund for the first 10 years on active duty).

What was your plan or dream for your life before meeting God on your Damascus Road?

What is God's calling on your life after you accepted God's free gift of salvation?

What do your doubters say about your changed and repurposed life?

Who came alongside to help you as God led you to a new purpose?

What life lessons or experiences in your old life helped you in your repurposed life?

When friends from the "old days" see you now, what surprises them most about your life?

Closing:

Most of us have had dreams for how we hoped or wanted our lives to go. Yet, due to circumstances of our own creation or from others, we found ourselves no longer moving in the direction we wanted for our lives. We were stuck with no real direction; not only were we no longer executing our plan, but we had also made decisions that had disqualified us from obtaining our dream. But what we see as disqualification, God sees as an opportunity for repurposing. If you are in need of God's repurposing, all you need to begin the process is to pray the prayer below.

Prayer:

Lord Jesus, thank you for making me a new creature in you. Thank you for taking me from my plans and repurposing me so I might serve you where you send me. I don't know everything you have planned in my new life or how you can and will use me, but help me be open and obedient to your leading. Even if what you want me to do is scary and intimidating, fill me with your strength and power. I desire to be strong and courageous for you, now and always, Amen!

NOTE PAGE

LESSON 5
RECYCLE: HOW GOD TURNS FAILURES INTO SOMETHING USABLE

Introduction: I was in grade school when the environmental movement began in the United States in the mid-1960s. I remember, even today, the early slogan of "Give a hoot, don't pollute." Whereas the Forest Service had Smokey the Bear, the environmentalists had the wise owl. It was time to clean up the brown clouds over places like Denver, Colorado or Los Angeles, California. Factories of all kinds were belching out chemicals into the air at alarming rates, with no regulations. Rivers and streams were clogged with discarded items as well as oil and other pollutants. I shudder when I remember how my parents and neighbors discarded old oil or household chemicals. I'm not sure when recycling came along, but I would ride my bike up and down the country roads picking up aluminum cans for recycling. I will admit, at nine years of age, I was more concerned with the money I received for the cans than for the environment I was saving.

Today, the commercials about recycling are more sophisticated. They will show how recycling an aluminum can helps build park benches. Or how recycled plastics are made into hundreds of useful products. I'm not sure there is a greeting card or bound book that is not made with some percentage of recycled paper. Though our recycling efforts could be better, we have come a long way in our efforts to make our environment safe and sustainable for future generations.

Today, we will take a close look at how God is in the recycling business with his people. It is encouraging to look back on some of my dismal failures to see how God recycled them into something new and usable.

In-depth Study:

Several years ago, my pastor did a series entitled Day of Decision. He intended to start in Genesis and go through the Bible, highlighting beloved characters and describing how they met their day of decision with victory or failure and then provide a current application. During this series, he invited me to preach several times. It was interesting because some of the most recognizable names in the Bible had resoundingly successful decisions followed by hugely disappointing ones. Moses, David, and Peter all come to mind as fitting this success/failure cycle quite well. The story of Moses is recorded throughout the books of Exodus, Leviticus, Numbers, and Deuteronomy. For this lesson, we will explore Moses' early life and how God recycles his life and uses him mightily.

Read Exodus 1 These are the names of the sons of Israel who went to Egypt with Jacob, each with his family: 2 Reuben, Simeon, Levi and Judah; 3 Issachar, Zebulun and Benjamin; 4 Dan and Naphtali; Gad and Asher. 5 The descendants of Jacob numbered seventy in all; Joseph was already in Egypt. 6 Now Joseph and all his brothers and all that generation died, 7 but the Israelites were exceedingly fruitful; they multiplied greatly, increased in numbers and became so numerous that the land was filled with them. 8 Then a new king, to whom Joseph meant nothing, came to power in Egypt. 9 "Look," he said to his people, "the Israelites have become far too numerous for us. 10 Come, we must deal shrewdly with them or they will become even more numerous and, if war breaks out, will join our enemies, fight against us and leave the country." 11 So they put slave masters over them to oppress them with forced labor, and they built Pithom and Ramesses as store cities for Pharaoh. 12 But the more they were oppressed, the more they multiplied and spread; so the Egyptians came to dread the Israelites 13 and worked them ruthlessly. 14 They made their lives bitter with harsh labor in brick and mortar and with all kinds of work in the fields; in all their harsh labor, the Egyptians worked them ruthlessly. 15 The king of Egypt said to the Hebrew midwives, whose names were Shiphrah and Puah, 16 "When you are helping the Hebrew women during childbirth on the delivery stool, if you see that the baby is a boy, kill him; but if it is a girl, let her live." 17 The midwives, however, feared God and did not do what the king of Egypt had told them to do; they let the boys live. 18 Then the king of Egypt summoned the midwives and asked them, "Why have you done this? Why have you let the boys live?" 19 The midwives answered Pharaoh, "Hebrew women are not like Egyptian women; they are vigorous and give birth before the midwives arrive." 20 So God was kind to the midwives and the people increased and became even more numerous. 21 And because the midwives feared God, he gave them families of their own. 22 Then Pharaoh gave this order to all his people: "Every Hebrew boy that is born you must throw into the Nile, but let every girl live."

Read Exodus 2 Now a man of the tribe of Levi married a Levite woman, 2 and she became pregnant and gave birth to a son. When she saw that he was a fine child, she hid him for three months. 3 But when she could hide him no longer, she got a papyrus basket for him and coated it with tar and pitch. She then placed the child in it and put it among the reeds along the bank of the Nile. 4 His sister stood at a distance to see what would happen to him. 5 Then Pharaoh's daughter went down to the Nile to bathe, and her attendants were walking along the riverbank. She saw the basket among the reeds and sent her female slave to get it. 6 She opened it and saw the baby. He was crying, and she felt sorry for him. "This is one of the Hebrew babies," she said. 7 Then his sister asked Pharaoh's daughter, "Shall I go and get one of the Hebrew women to nurse the baby for you?" 8 "Yes, go," she answered. So the girl went and got the baby's mother. 9 Pharaoh's daughter said to her, "Take this baby and nurse him for me, and I will pay you." So the woman took the baby and nursed him. 10 When the child grew older, she took him to Pharaoh's daughter and he became her son. She named him Moses, saying, "I drew him out of the water." 11 One day, after Moses had grown up, he went out to where his own people were and watched them at their hard labor. He saw an Egyptian beating a Hebrew, one of his own people. 12 Looking this way and that and seeing no one, he killed the Egyptian and hid him in the sand. 13 The next day he went out and saw two Hebrews fighting. He asked the one in the wrong, "Why are you hitting your fellow Hebrew?" 14 The man said, "Who made you ruler and judge over us? Are you thinking of killing me as you killed the Egyptian?" Then Moses was afraid and thought, "What I did must have become known." 15 When Pharaoh heard of this, he tried to kill Moses, but Moses fled from Pharaoh and went to live in Midian, where he sat down by a well. 16 Now a priest of Midian had seven daughters, and they came to draw water and fill the troughs to water their father's flock. 17 Some shepherds came along and drove them away, but Moses got up and came to their rescue and watered their flock. 18 When the girls returned to Reuel, their father asked them, "Why have you returned so early today?" 19 They answered, "An Egyptian rescued us from the shepherds. He even drew water for us and watered the flock." 20 "And where is he?" Reuel asked his daughters. "Why did you leave him? Invite him to have something to eat." 21 Moses agreed to stay with the man, who gave his daughter Zipporah to Moses in marriage. 22 Zipporah gave birth to a son, and Moses named him Gershom, saying, "I have become a foreigner in a foreign land." 23 During that long period, the king of Egypt died. The Israelites groaned in their slavery and cried out, and their cry for help because of their slavery went up to God. 24 God heard their groaning and he remembered his covenant with Abraham, with Isaac and with Jacob. 25 So God looked on the Israelites and was concerned about them.

To understand the setting, one needs to know that through several incidents that go under the heading "they meant it for evil, but God intended it for good," (Genesis 50:20) the Hebrew people moved to Egypt where they prospered and multiplied in numbers. Then we find that "there arose up a new king over Egypt, which knew not Joseph." (Exodus 1:8, KJV)

Everything changed. The new king was terrified of the Hebrews' numbers and allegiance. His first plan was to work them to death through slavery. When that proved unsuccessful, he told the midwives to kill all the Hebrew male babies at birth. The midwives refused to obey the Pharaoh's decree because they feared God, telling the Pharaoh that the Hebrew women delivered more quickly than Egyptian women and would deliver before they arrived. Finally, the Pharoah ordered all infant boys born to the Hebrews to be thrown into the Nile River.

Why did the midwives not adhere to the Pharaoh's command to kill all the Hebrews' baby boys?

Explain a situation where you circumvented a rule or law because it was unjust or against God's word.

A Levite couple gave birth to a baby boy. When the parents could no longer hide him, the mother made a waterproof basket, placed her baby into it, and then placed him carefully in the Nile. Miriam, the baby's older sister, kept track of the basket and intervened when the Pharaoh's daughter found the basket and saw the baby. Miriam volunteered to get a Hebrew mother to nurse the baby. The baby was returned temporarily to his parents, where he lived until he was weaned. Then he was returned to Pharaoh's daughter.

What name did the Pharaoh's daughter give the baby in the basket? Why was it appropriate?

Moses grew up in the palace of the Pharaoh and was "educated in all the wisdom of the Egyptians and was powerful in speech and action" (Acts 7:22). At age 40, Moses decided to go check on the Hebrew people. He watched their hard labor and observed an Egyptian beating a Hebrew slave.

Obviously, Moses was enraged at this sight. He looked to see if anyone was watching what he was doing. When he believed no one was observing him, he killed the Egyptian and buried his body in the sand.

What is Moses' reaction to the mistreatment of the Hebrew slave?

How did his actions influence his life?

What happened when Moses confronted two Hebrew men fighting later?

What happened when Pharaoh heard his adopted Hebrew grandson had killed an Egyptian?

Moses fled to Midian. He lived in exile for forty years. During that time, he met Jethro (also referred to as Reuel) and his seven daughters. Eventually, he married Zipporah and had two sons. Moses became a shepherd for Jethro's flocks.

As a shepherd, Moses learned how to protect the sheep, how to find the best pastures, and how to find water. He learned to survive in the desert. As a shepherd, Moses most likely learned the importance of being present, persistence, and patience; sheep don't always do what is in their best interest or go in a direction that is safe. The rest of the Exodus story proves the Hebrew people were a lot like sheep. Going any which way and not always doing what was in their best interest.

What life lessons did Moses gain while in exile in Midian?

How would these life lessons prepare him for what God was about to call him to do?

Read Exodus 3 (ESV) Now Moses was keeping the flock of his father-in-law, Jethro, the priest of Midian, and he led his flock to the west side of the wilderness and came to Horeb, the mountain of God. 2 And the angel of the Lord appeared to him in a flame of fire out of the midst of a bush. He looked, and behold, the bush was burning, yet it was not consumed. 3 And Moses said, "I will turn aside to see this great sight, why the bush is not burned." 4 When the Lord saw that he turned aside to see, God called to him out of the bush, "Moses, Moses!" And he said, "Here I am." 5 Then he said, "Do not come near; take your sandals off your feet, for the place on which you are standing is holy ground." 6 And he said, "I am the God of your father, the God of Abraham, the God of Isaac, and the God of Jacob." And Moses hid his face, for he was afraid to look at God. 7 Then the Lord said, "I have surely seen the affliction of my people who are in Egypt and have heard their cry because of their taskmasters. I know their sufferings, 8 and I have come down to deliver them out of the hand of the Egyptians and to bring them up out of that land to a good and broad land, a land flowing with milk and honey, to the place of the Canaanites, the Hittites, the Amorites, the Perizzites, the Hivites, and the Jebusites. 9 And now, behold, the cry of the people of Israel has come to me, and I have also seen the oppression with which the Egyptians oppress them. 10 Come, I will send you to Pharaoh that you may bring my people, the children of Israel, out of Egypt." 11 But Moses said to God, "Who am I that I should go to Pharaoh and bring the children of Israel out of Egypt?" 12 He said, "But I will be with you, and this shall be the sign for you, that I have sent you: when you have brought the people out of Egypt, you shall serve God on this mountain." 13 Then Moses said to God, "If I come to the people of Israel and say to them, 'The God of your fathers has sent me to you,' and they ask me, 'What is his name?' what shall I say to them?" 14 God said to Moses, "I am who I am." And he said, "Say this to the people of Israel: 'I am has sent me to you.'" 15 God also said to Moses, "Say this to the people of Israel: 'The Lord, the God of your fathers, the God of Abraham, the God of Isaac, and the God of Jacob, has sent me to you.' This is my name forever, and thus I am to be remembered throughout all generations. 16 Go and gather the elders of Israel together and say to them, 'The Lord, the God of your fathers, the God of Abraham, of Isaac, and of Jacob, has appeared to me, saying, "I have observed you and what has been done to you in Egypt, 17 and I promise that I will bring you up out of the affliction of Egypt to the land of the Canaanites, the Hittites, the Amorites, the Perizzites, the Hivites, and the Jebusites, a land flowing with milk and honey." 18 And they will listen to your voice, and you and the elders of Israel shall go to the king of Egypt and say to him, 'The Lord, the God of the Hebrews, has met with us; and now, please let us go a three days' journey into the wilderness, that we may sacrifice to the Lord our God.' 19 But I know that the king of Egypt will not let you go unless compelled by a mighty hand. 20 So I will stretch out my hand and strike Egypt with all the wonders that I will do in it; after that, he will let you go. 21 And I will give this people favor in the sight of the Egyptians; and when you go, you shall not go empty, 22 but each woman shall ask of her neighbor, and any woman who lives in her house, for silver and gold jewelry, and for clothing. You shall put them on your sons and on your daughters. So you shall plunder the Egyptians."

Read Exodus 4:1-17 (ESV) Then Moses answered, "But behold, they will not believe me or listen to my voice, for they will say, 'The Lord did not appear to you.'" 2 The Lord said to him, "What is that in your hand?" He said, "A staff." 3 And he said, "Throw it on the ground." So he threw it on the ground, and it became a serpent, and Moses ran from it. 4 But the Lord said to Moses, "Put out your hand and catch it by the tail" so he put out his hand and caught it, and it became a staff in his hand 5 "that they may believe that the Lord, the God of their fathers, the God of Abraham, the God of Isaac, and the God of Jacob, has appeared to you." 6 Again, the Lord said to him, "Put your hand inside your cloak." And he put his hand inside his cloak, and when he took it out, behold, his hand was leprous like snow. 7 Then God said, "Put your hand back inside your cloak." So he put his hand back inside his cloak, and when he took it out, behold, it was restored like the rest of his flesh. 8 "If they will not believe you," God said, "or listen to the first sign, they may believe the latter sign. 9 If they will not believe even these two signs or listen to your voice, you shall take some water from the Nile and pour it on the dry ground, and the water that you shall take from the Nile will become blood on the dry ground." 10 But Moses said to the Lord, "Oh, my Lord, I am not eloquent, either in the past or since you have spoken to your servant, but I am slow of speech and of tongue." 11 Then the Lord said to him, "Who has made man's mouth? Who makes him mute, or deaf, or seeing, or blind? Is it not I, the Lord? 12 Now therefore go, and I will be with your mouth and teach you what you shall speak." 13 But he said, "Oh, my Lord, please send someone else." 14 Then the anger of the Lord was kindled against Moses and he said, "Is there not Aaron, your brother, the Levite? I know that he can speak well. Behold, he is coming out to meet you, and when he sees you, he will be glad in his heart. 15 You shall speak to him and put the words in his mouth, and I will be with your mouth and with his mouth and will teach you both what to do. 16 He shall speak for you to the people, and he shall be your mouth, and you shall be as God to him. 17 And take in your hand this staff, with which you shall do the signs."

Where was Moses when he saw the burning bush?

How did God address Moses as he approached the burning bush?

How did God identify Himself?

What were the circumstances of the Hebrew people at this time?

What was God calling Moses to do?

God was calling Moses to be his man to lead the Hebrews out of slavery to the land God had promised Abraham more than 400 years earlier (Genesis 15:13-14)

List the four excuses Moses gave God for not being the right person for the job.

List the answers God provided for each of Moses' excuses.

How do you reconcile Exodus 4:10 with Stephen's summary of Moses's biography in Acts 7:22?

Application:

Moses was from the tribe of Levi, and his life was spared when the Pharaoh ordered the genocide of Hebrew male babies. Yet, even with his privileged upbringing in Pharaoh's palace, he murdered an Egyptian. He then fled Egypt and started a new life in Midian. He married and had two sons. However, he totally left his life in Midian when God chose to recycle the events of his life and used him to free God's people from slavery in Egypt and return them to the land God had promised Abraham 400 years before.

The rest of Moses' life was spent bringing the people out of slavery and into the nation to be known as the Israelites. It was not a smooth transition for the people or for their leader Moses.

List events in your life that you believed would limit you from accomplishing God's calling on your life.

How did God's transformational love and grace recycle the above roadblock(s) for his purpose?

Since God recycled you from the above event(s), what is God's call on your life?

What excuse(s) do you give for not stepping into God's call for your life?

What signs, scriptures, or people did God provide that showed you he was indeed calling you?

How did God's recycling of your life change your work in his kingdom?

Closing:

Moses was set apart from birth for God's service; however, when he killed the Egyptian and was later confronted with this murder by another Hebrew, it seemed the only thing left was for Moses to flee from both the Pharaoh and the Hebrew people. Whatever calling God had on Moses' life appeared to be voided by his actions; however, God was not finished with Moses. God used Moses' desert dwelling and shepherding around Midian to recycle him into his instrument to return the people of Israel to the land he had promised Abraham centuries before. God is not only the Master Restorer, but he is the master at recycling. All he wants from us is an openness to be utilized for his kingdom.

If you are ready to accept God's call on your life to be recycled for his purpose, start with this simple prayer.

Prayer:

God, you are always ready with your love and grace to recycle me into the servant you desire. Help me open myself to the reality that you can take that which has been discarded by the world as broken and unusable and use it in a mighty way. Through you, my recycling into your instrument can and will make eternal differences in others. I give you permission to transform me, starting today.

Guide me this day to continue in your word, fellowshipping with your people, and following your plan for my life. When I fail, take my failures and hurts, recycle them into something usable for your kingdom. Amen!

NOTE PAGE

NOTE PAGE

AFTERWORD

This study came about due to my realizing there are no "honorable mention" lives in God's eyes. In Luke chapters 7-8 there are various stories related about people who encountered Jesus, as they were, and they were forever changed. The centurion who believed Jesus could heal his servant even from afar, and Jesus did. Changing both the centurion's and his servant's lives. Then there was the widow's only son who died. Jesus had compassion on her and touched the young man's coffin and told him to get up, which he did. Again, lives changed for both the widow and her son, and all those who were witnesses to the event. Jesus was with his disciples as they crossed the lake when a storm threatened to swamp the boat; the disciples cried out and the wind and waves obeyed Jesus who calmed the storm. Again, faith was increased by those who saw Jesus' power. In the Gerasenes, a demon-possessed man cried out to Jesus, afraid of what he might do. Jesus exorcised the demons and put them in the herd of pigs which ran off a cliff and died. After that, the man was in his right mind, calm, and dressed appropriately. When the members of the town saw him, they wanted no part of Jesus and asked him to leave them. Yet the man who was relieved from demon possession and was restored, wanted to follow Jesus. Jesus told him to stay and share his testimony with the people. Again, one man is forever changed and others are introduced to God's transformational grace and love.

Over the course of this study, you have explored how God's transformational love and grace can redeem, restore, repurpose, and recycle your life into something beautiful and useful in his kingdom. You studied how God chose to redeem us through his Son, Jesus, in Lesson 1. The redeeming theme continued in Lesson 2 as you looked at the cycle of God's love, grace, and mercy as we live our faith in a world always trying to trip us up. In Lessons 3-5 you explored the lives of sentinel men of faith. David, who was restored after a sordid affair and the murder of one of his mighty men, in order to hide his sin. Next, you saw how God took Saul the zealot against Christianity and repurposed that zeal as he became the great missionary to the Gentiles. Finally, the study examined the life of Moses, whom God recycled into a leader of the great exodus from Egypt to the promised land. Each of these men encountered God in such a way that they were never the same. God used them in ways they could not fathom due to their moral failures. They are great examples of what God can and will do for you if you believe and are faithful.

My prayer at the beginning of this study was that you would seek to encounter God's transformational love and grace, that you would enter this study seeking transparency with God and yourself. In the study, questions were asked related to the biblical texts and also personal inquiries for you to wrestle with for clarity and growth. I hope each of you indeed grew through your time in God's word and your reflection of this study.

If you are still struggling with questions of redemption or how God can use you, I hope you will reach out to a Christian friend or your pastor who can help you explore your questions and struggles in order that you continue to grow in your faith. God is not finished with you yet and will continue to redeem, restore, repurpose and recycle you as needed for you to serve him.

Thank you for your faithful study and participation in this work; may God continue to transform you in your faith journey.

9 781969 506710